This edition published by Parragon Books Ltd in 2015

Parragon Books Ltd
Chartist House
15–17 Trim Street
Bath BA1 1HA, UK
www.parragon.com

ISBN 978-1-4723-9032-5

Printed in China

Disney Junior COLLECTION

Contents

PaRragon

Bath • New York • Cologne • Melbourne • Delhi
Hong Kong • Shenzhen • Singapore • Amsterdam

MICKEY MOUSE CLUBHOUSE

UP, UP AND AWAY!

By **Sheila Sweeny Higginson**
Illustrated by the **Disney Storybook Artists**
Designed by **Elizabeth Andaluz**

Donald and his friends were standing outside the Clubhouse on a crisp, bright day.

"Oh, Donald," Daisy said, "look at the sky! It's lovely!"

"Shhh!" Donald whispered. "Don't make a move! Something is following me and I'm going to find out who - or what - it is!"

Daisy giggled as she looked behind Donald. "Oh, my!" she said. "There *is* something following you! It's wearing a sailor's cap – just like yours. It's got cute webbed feet – just like yours. And when you move, it moves, too."

"Aw, phooey," Donald quacked as he turned round and saw ... his shadow! "That is a fine-looking shape, but I still don't trust it!"

Donald glared at his shadow.

"Cheer up, buddy," Mickey said. "Why don't you leave your shadow on the ground and come with me?"

"I don't know," Donald said, moping. "Where are we going?"

"Up, up and away!" Mickey cheered. "Who wants to help Minnie and me fly our hot-air balloon?"

"I sure do!" shouted Goofy.

"You can count me out," Donald grumbled.
"I don't trust that thing. Besides," he added,
"I'm not missing lunch."

"Aw, come on, Donald," Minnie pleaded.
"I've packed a square meal for each of us.
Up, up and away!"

Donald finally agreed to go with
his friends.

"Something's wrong," Mickey said. "The balloon won't fill with air!"

"That's too bad, buddy," said Donald, trying to hide a grin. "I guess we'll just have to go back to the Clubhouse for lunch."

"Oh, Toodles!" Mickey said. "Do we have a Mousketool that can help?" Toodles appeared. "Do any of you know how we can use this?" Mickey asked his friends.

"I know, Mickey!" answered Minnie. "We can turn the handle to inflate the balloon with hot air."

"Why, you're right, Minnie!" Mickey shouted.
"We've got ears! Say cheers!"

Soon, the friends were floating high in the sky.
"Up, up and away!" cried Daisy. "This is fun!"
"Look, everyone!" yelled Minnie. "Can you see the Clubhouse from here? It looks so small! And there are so many shapes below us. I see a heart and a rectangle. What do you see?"

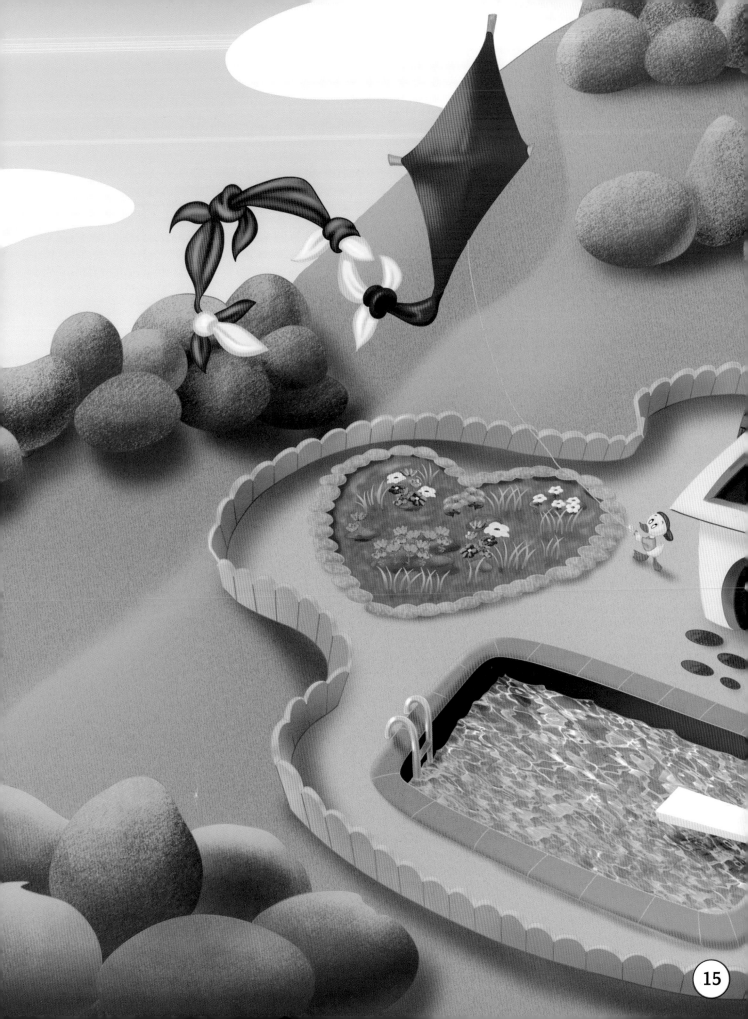

"I see a triangle!" Mickey said. "And there are Chip and Dale playing a round of golf!"

"It should be called a triangle of golf," laughed Daisy. "Just look at all those triangle-shaped flags!"

"What's a triangle?" asked Goofy, as he bit into his sandwich.

"A triangle is a shape with three sides that all have points at the ends – sort of like your sandwich," Minnie explained.

"Or like that?" Goofy questioned, as he pointed to a huge triangle in front of the balloon. It was the top of a mountain!

Suddenly, a gust of wind whisked the friends right towards it!

"We need help," cried Mickey. "Oh, Toodles!"

Toodles appeared with a triangle, a patch, a ladder and a spyglass.

"Which tool should we use?" asked Minnie.

"Let's try them all!" said Mickey. "Daisy, ring the triangle for help!" Daisy rang the triangle, but it didn't help them get off the mountain.

"Minnie, patch the hole!" cried Mickey. Minnie put a square patch on the round hole in the balloon, but it was too small.

"Goofy, look through the spyglass!" shouted Mickey. Goofy held the spyglass and saw that the ground looked very far away.

"There's only one tool left," yelled Mickey. "To the ladder!"

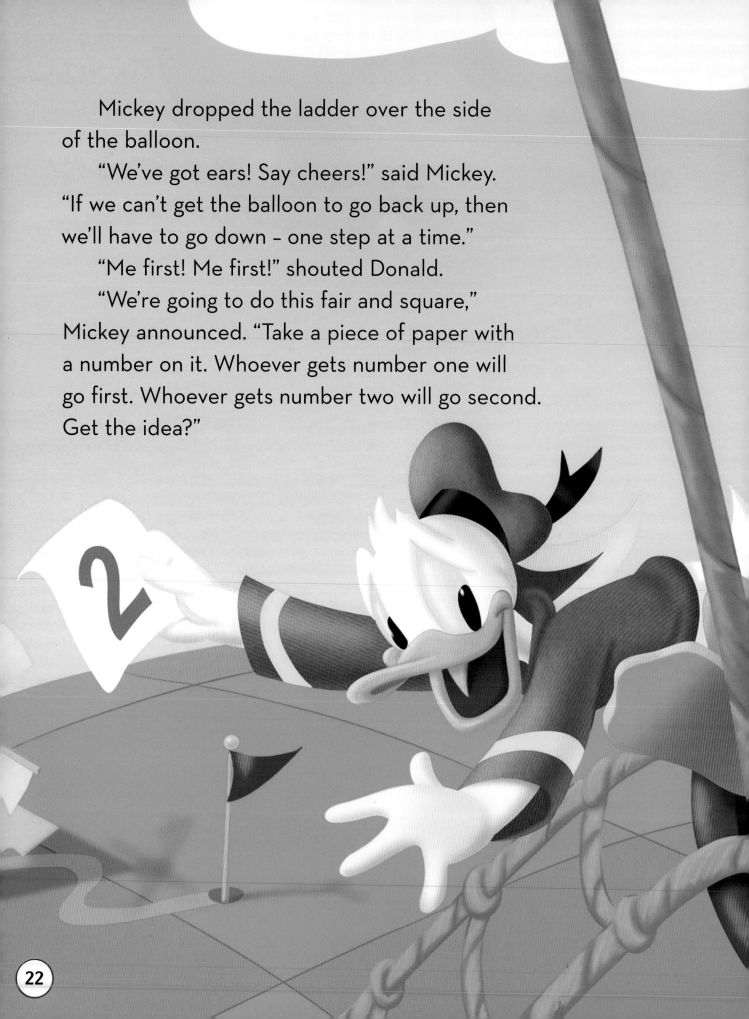

Mickey dropped the ladder over the side of the balloon.

"We've got ears! Say cheers!" said Mickey. "If we can't get the balloon to go back up, then we'll have to go down – one step at a time."

"Me first! Me first!" shouted Donald.

"We're going to do this fair and square," Mickey announced. "Take a piece of paper with a number on it. Whoever gets number one will go first. Whoever gets number two will go second. Get the idea?"

The friends climbed down the ladder one by one. Everyone was happy to be standing on firm ground again. "We're in great shape, unlike our balloon," said Mickey. "But we're going to have to hike back home. It's not far – just down that path … or maybe it's that other one…."

The friends trudged along, growing more and more tired.
"I think we've been walking in circles," Mickey finally said.
"I'm sure I've seen this tree before."

The friends needed help to get back to the Clubhouse. "Oh, Toodles!" Mickey called.

Toodles appeared, showing three pictures of Mickey.

Mickey shared them with his friends: "I'm standing in front of the Clubhouse and my shadow is different in each picture. In the morning, my shadow falls in front of me. At noon, I have no shadow. In the evening, my shadow falls behind me. Do any of you know what this could mean?"

"I've got it!" Donald shouted. "Right now, it's late and the sun is setting behind us. Toodles shows that in the evening, our shadows point towards the Clubhouse. If we follow them, they'll lead us back home."

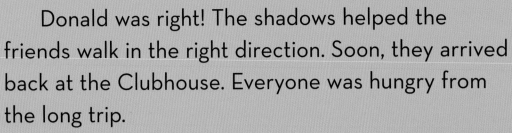

Donald was right! The shadows helped the friends walk in the right direction. Soon, they arrived back at the Clubhouse. Everyone was hungry from the long trip.

"Well, Donald," Daisy said, "do you trust your shadow now?"

"I'll trust the handsome guy to lead me home," Donald answered. "But he better not ask me to share my sandwich!"

The End

Peck's Trail Mix Mix-up

Based on the episode written by **Mike Kramer**
Adapted by **Annie Auerbach**
Illustrated by **Marco Bucci**

One day, Sheriff Callie spots her deputy walking down the street.

   "Howdy, Peck!" she says. "Goin' to get your weekly shipment of trail mix?"

   "Sure am, Sheriff," Deputy Peck replies. "You know how much I love my trail mix!"

Just then, Cody races up, swirling dust behind him.

"Mail!" he announces, reaching into his bag. Cody gives out letters, packages, a ball of string for Callie and, of course, Peck's prized package.

"Hoo-wee!" cheers Peck, hugging his trail mix. "Thanks, Cody!"

Uh-oh! Peck's badge pokes a hole in the bag. As Peck wanders off, he doesn't notice he's leaving a line of trail mix behind him!

Sheriff Callie and Deputy Peck walk into Ella's Saloon.

"Two glasses of milk, please, Ella," says Callie.

"Comin' right up!" says Ella. But when she tries to open a new milk bottle, she needs help. "Deputy Peck, I hate to ask while you're eating your trail mix, but...."

"'Duty before deliciousness' I always say," Peck tells her with a smile. "Besides, it'll just mean more for later."

So Peck gives each milk-bottle cap a rat-a-tat-tat with his beak to take them off.

"Now, hold on a cotton-pickin' minute," Peck says when he returns to his stool. "Has anyone been eating my trail mix?"

"Um, you mean like you?" says his pal, Toby.

"No, I mean anybody but me. This here bag's not as full as when I came in here," Peck replies.

"You're the only one that's been eatin' it, Peck," says Callie. "Maybe you had more than you thought."

Figuring the sheriff is probably right, Peck decides to head out and do his deputy rounds.

"I want to come!" says Toby. "Can I? Can I?"

"Of course, my prickly pal," replies Peck. "See you later, folks."

Toby, Peck and his beloved trail mix head outside.

Peck always likes helping out. As soon as he sees Priscilla struggling to lift a heavy basket, he hurries over to help.

When Doc Quackers can't get a wheel to stay on his wagon, Peck quickly offers to do it for him.

As Toby and Peck head back to the jailhouse, Peck still has no idea about the hole in his bag of trail mix!

Sheriff Callie is at her desk when Peck and Toby walk in.
"Is everything in Nice and Friendly Corners still nice and friendly?"
she asks.

"Sure is," replies Peck. "And I believe I need a snack!"

But when he puts the bag on the desk, he gasps. "My trail mix! Now it's half empty!"

"Are you sure you didn't eat that much?" asks Callie.

"Positive!" says Peck. "And I never let that bag out of my hands!"

"Sure you did," Toby says. "You set it down at Priscilla's house and also by Doc's wagon."

"Flyin' feathers, you're right!" exclaims Peck. "Which can only mean one thing: somebody is stealing my trail mix!"

"Now, Peck, don't go blamin' folks before you know all the facts," warns Callie. "There could be another reason why it's missin'."

But Peck is too upset to listen. "Yeah, the reason is someone's stealin' it so they can eat it! I'm going to get to the bottom of this. I'm going to catch me a thief!"

Peck goes back to all the places he visited that day. But instead of finding out who ate his trail mix, he just blames everyone for stealing it.

"Maybe you need to gather more facts, Deputy," suggests Doc.

Just then, Peck looks down and sees a line of trail mix.

"My trail mix!" he cries. "The thief is spillin' it everywhere. If we follow this trail, I bet it'll lead straight to him. Come on!"

Peck, Callie and Toby follow the trail mix all the way back to the jailhouse.

"Well, bend my beak," says Peck. "This thief is sneakier than I thought!"

"He's been stealing your trail mix from under our very noses!" Toby says.

Peck sets a trap inside the jail cell.

"Here's how it works," begins Peck. "When the thief comes to steal my trail mix, he'll move the bag, which will pull the string and shut the door."

Toby and Peck think it's a great idea, but Sheriff Callie isn't sure.

Then she spots the hole in the trail mix bag. "Sweet sassafras, Peck! Look! Your bag has a —"

But Peck's not listening. "We've got to be quiet or the thief won't come," he says as he ushers Callie and Toby out of the door. "You two leave so the thief thinks the place is empty."

Callie chuckles to herself. She realizes Peck will have to figure this one out alone. "All righty," she says. "Give me a holler if you need me."

When Peck is alone, he hides behind the desk to wait for the thief. Before long, he hears a tap, tap, tap.

Peck doesn't realize that it's the sound of the trail mix slowly spilling out of the bag and hitting the floor!

He tiptoes into the jail cell and looks around for the thief. But then he trips on the string and ... *SLAM!* The door closes and locks him in jail!

"Sheriff, help!" he yells.

Callie and Toby rush in to see what's happened.

"I heard the thief," explains Peck. "So I snuck in here after him. But the crook escaped before I even saw him!"

Callie unlocks the cell door and goes inside. "Peck, I know who the culprit is," she says, picking up the leaking bag. "It's this hole!"

"Well, I'll be...." Peck says. "That means my trail mix was leaking out of the bag the whole time."

Peck drops his head, feeling ashamed. "And here was me thinking it was one of my friends. That wasn't very nice and friendly."

Callie puts a hand on Peck's shoulder. "Nope, but we all make mistakes."

"I wish there was some way I could make it up to everybody," Peck says. Then he brightens. "Now, hold on — there is!"

The next day when the mail comes in, Cody is confused. "Why the extra-large bag of trail mix this time?" he asks Peck.

Peck smiles. "Because I'm going to share it with all my friends! I'm sorry I blamed y'all for takin' my trail mix. Next time, I'll get all the facts before I open my beak."

Callie nods. "Now that's a nice and friendly promise, Peck!"

Peck opens the new bag of trail mix. "Come on, everybody. Let's eat!"

The End

MICKEY MOUSE CLUBHOUSE

FUN ACTIVITIES!

Hi, there! Do you want to come to my Clubhouse?
Just colour me in and say, "Meeska, Mooska, Mickey Mouse!"

Here it is – the Clubhouse! Colour it in and come on inside!

Colour this picture of the kitchen. It has an oven, a sink and a ... leaping frog! Hey, what's he doing here?

Let's follow the leaping frog to the garden. How many bees
do you see in the picture? Circle the number.

1 2 3 4 5 6 7 8 9 10

Answer:

Pluto and the frog are playing a game. It's called 'leapfrog'.
Who is hopping higher? Colour them in.

Can you help Pluto find the frog in this picture?
Then colour in the picture.

Daisy has found the frog!
Colour this picture of the frog in her basket.

Match the leaping frog to its shadow.

57

Come on back to the Clubhouse. It looks like Daisy needs help getting ready for a surprise party! Colour this picture.

Daisy and Mickey blew up all these balloons!
Find two that are exactly the same and colour them in.

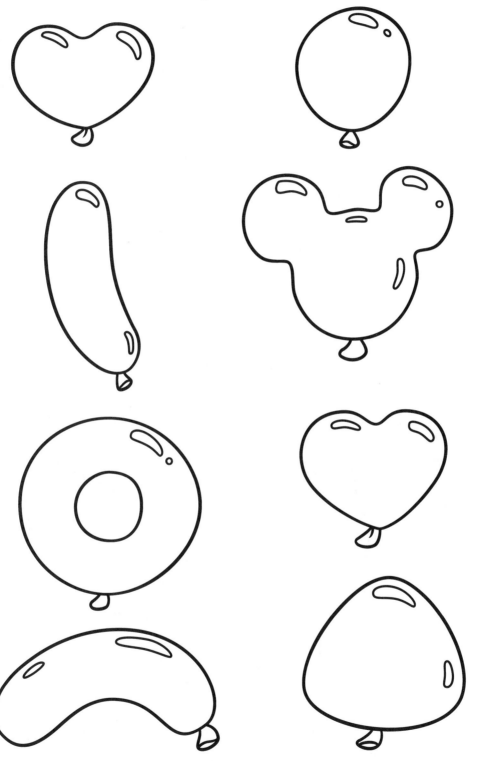

Answer:

Daisy is baking a cake. How many eggs is she using?
Circle the number.

1 2 3 4 5 6 7 8 9 10

Answer:

2

The cake is finished! You can help to decorate it.
Draw four candles on top of the cake.

It is time for some ice cream! Draw three scoops
in Minnie's cone, then colour in the picture.

Now Daisy and Donald are sharing a banana split.
How many spoons are in the picture?

Answer:

2

'Pin the Tail on the Donkey' is Goofy's favourite party game.
He is trying to put the tail in the right place.

Now it's your turn! Draw a tail on this donkey.

It's getting late and the guests are leaving the party. Oh, Toodles!
Which of these objects will help them to find their way in the dark?
Point to the correct object.

Answer:

The torch.

Who has Donald found hiding on the path?

It's time for an out-of-this-world adventure! Colour this picture of Goofy blasting off to outer space! Go, Goofy!

Help Goofy get to Mars – draw a path through the maze.

Answer:

How many planets are in Goofy's path?

Circle the number, then colour in the picture.

1 2 3 4 5 6 7 8 9 10

Answer:

Three of these spaceships look the same.

Goofy's spaceship is different. Can you find Goofy's ship?

Answer:

Goofy needs help getting down from his spaceship.

Which Mouseketool should he use? Point to the correct object.

Answer:

The slide.

Goofy has invited four aliens back to the Clubhouse!
Colour this picture of Goofy and his new friends.

Draw a line to match each alien to its shadow.

74

Welcome to the Clubhouse garden! Colour this picture of Minnie and Daisy doing some gardening.

Minnie has taken some photographs in the garden.
How many pictures are there? Circle the number.

1 2 3 4 5 6 7 8 9 10

Answer:

Minnie is picking some flowers to make a bunch.
Help her by colouring in the flowers.

Colour in this picture of Daisy wearing a flower chain!

Can you find one tree, two sunflowers, three birds, four bees and five friends in this picture? Circle them as you find them.

Answers:

Draw a line to match each picture with the correct number.

1

2

3

4

5

We're having a great day at the zoo! Write how many legs each animal has on the ground.

Answers:

Write the numbers one to five to put these zoo animals
in size order, from smallest to biggest.

_____

_____

_____

_____

_____

Answer:

The seal pond is Pluto's favourite place at the zoo.
The seals are throwing a ball.

The monkeys are swinging from the branches.

Draw a line to match each animal to its shadow.

Answers:

Help Goofy through the maze to find his way to the penguins.

What a great day! Now I want to read a book.
Colour in Mickey's story time.

It's bedtime! That means it's time for me to put my book away.

TREASURE HUNT ACTIVITIES!

Join Jake's pirate crew – draw yourself as a pirate.

Remember to add these pirate items.

spyglass   eye patch

compass   sword

coin purse   pirate hat

Now that you're part of the pirate crew,
it's time to go to Pirate Island!
Which line on the map leads there?
Remember: 'X' marks the spot!

Answer:

Every pirate crew needs ... a hideout!

Look at these two pictures of the hideout.

Find and circle five differences.

Colour in a skull and crossbones every time you find a difference.

Answers:

You're up in the hideout's crow's nest with Jake.
Which of these ships is the Jolly Roger? Circle it and say,
"The Jolly Roger be heading this way!"

Answer:

How many times can you find the word PIRATE in this
wordsearch? Circle the words as you find them.

X M Y N O P E P

P P I R A T E I

I O I B A I I R

R U X R R W R A

A R U T A O Q T

T P P I R A T E

E E E R A K L Y

P I R A T E I N

94

How many Gold Doubloons has the pirate crew earned?
Count them!

Answer:

9

Colour in the sneaky snook, Captain Hook!

Yo-ho, way to go!
Colour in Jake, Izzy, Cubby and Skully.

Draw a line to match the pirates to their property.

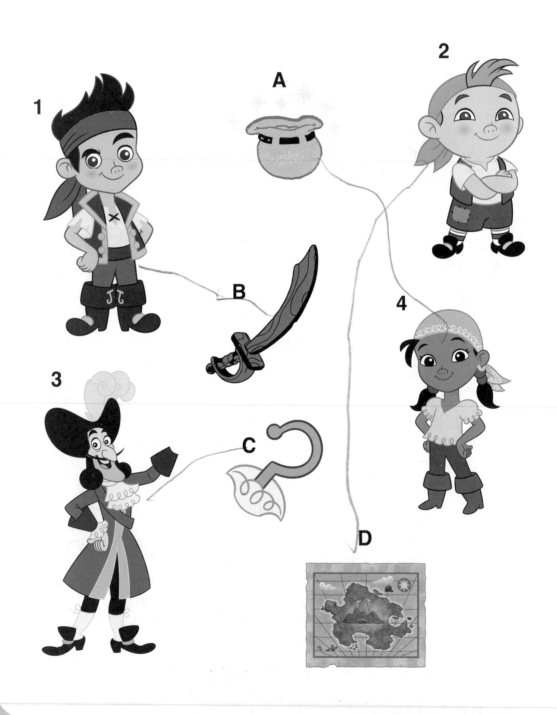

1

A

2

B

4

3

C

D

Answers:

All shipshape and seaworthy pirates have their own skull and crossbones.

This is Jake's:

This is Captain Hook's:

Draw your own skull and crossbones.

Avast! This be the skull and crossbones of ....Daniel.................

Shiver me timbers! Captain Hook is spying on
Jake and his pirate crew. Colour in the pesky pirate.

Jake has noticed that something odd has washed up on the beach.... Look at the two pictures below – can you spy the difference?

Answer:

Jake and his crew want to return Hook's hat
to him because it's the right thing to do.
Can you guide Bucky and the pirate crew
through the maze to the Jolly Roger?

Colour in this spyglass
and keep a lookout!

Where's the best place
to be on the lookout?

C l o w s n e s t.

The Jolly Roger has been spotted near Skull Rock. Let's check Cubby's map. Can you circle Skull Rock?

Can you point to the four points of the compass?

What's that sound? Tick Tock Croc! Colour him!

Help Jake climb up the rope net to get aboard the Jolly Roger.
Use the key to move through the maze.

Key:

Move Left   Move Up

Finish

Start

Answer:

Hook is happy to have his hat back, but he wishes those scallywags hadn't had so much fun returning it! Join the dots and colour in Captain Hook's hat.

It's Skully's birthday and Jake, Izzy and Cubby
are throwing him a party.
Draw a present for Skully below.

Skully's joke corner:
Q: What do pirates ask when
someone leaves a door open?
A: Were you born in a barn-acle?

Look at the picture of Skully's party and answer the questions below.

1. How many party hats can you count? ___4___

2. Circle the correct sentence.

(Jake is wearing a headscarf.)   Jake is wearing a neckscarf.

3. Who has a bag of pixie dust around her neck? __iss,__

4. Jake, Izzy and Cubby are children. Skully is a __parot__ .

Answers:
1 – 4;
2 – headscarf;
3 – Izzy;
4 – parrot.

107

Write your own pirate adventure and draw pictures to match in these boxes. The first story box has been done for you.

1. It's Skully's birthday. Jake and the crew have planned a party. But, oh, no! Captain Hook has stolen all Skully's presents!

2.

3.

Hints and tips:
- Make sure your story has a beginning, a middle and an end.
- Who are the characters in your story?
- Where is the story taking place?
- What is happening in your story?

Remember: there's no limit to your imagination, so get creative!

4.

5.

Skully's joke corner:

Q: How much does a pirate pay for a peg leg and a hook?

A: An arm and a leg!

6.

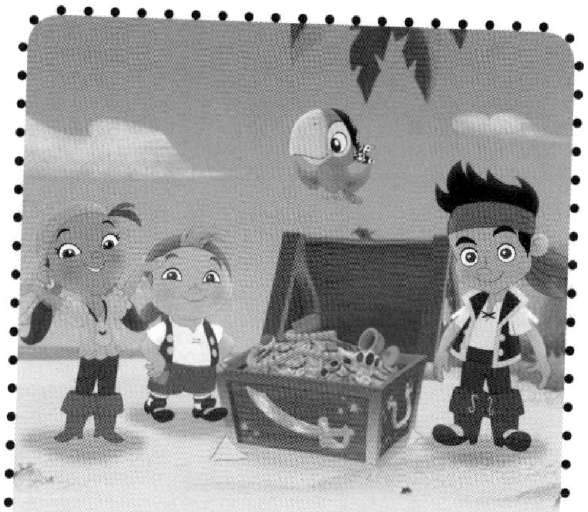

Take it in turns with a friend to connect two of the dots with a line. If your line completes a square, put your initial in it. Continue until all the dots are joined up. The player with the most boxes is the winner!

Grab a piratey friend and decide which of you is going to be Jake and which of you is going to be Hook. Take it in turns to draw either a sword (for Jake) or a hook (for Hook). The first player to get three in a row is the winner!

Captain Hook and Mr Smee have taken Skully's presents to Shipwreck Rock. How will Jake and the crew get them back?

Cross out every 'A' to discover the answer and copy the remaining letters on to the lines below.

AFAALAY WAAIATAH IAAZAZAAYAAS PAIAAXAIAE ADUASAAT

_ _ _   _ _ _ _   _ _ _ _ _ ,

_ _ _ _ _   _ _ _ _.

Answer: FLY WITH IZZY'S PIXIE DUST.

112

Hooray! The pirate crew can finally have a party for Skully!
Complete the scene by giving everyone a party hat,
then colour them in!

Jake's sword was given to him by Peter Pan so he
could be a good leader. Are you a good leader, too?
Draw your pirate sword below.

Oh, no! That sneaky snook Captain Hook has stolen Jake's sword. Can you find it below?

Answer:

Jake and the crew are chasing Captain Hook and
Mr Smee because they've stolen Jake's sword. Guide Jake
through the maze to get his sword back.

Answer:

Jake and the pirate crew have followed Captain Hook
to a canyon, but Hook has pushed the log bridge into
the canyon, so they can't cross. Izzy has a plan ...
they can use her pixie dust to fly over!

1. Which of these pictures shows Izzy using her pixie dust? _____

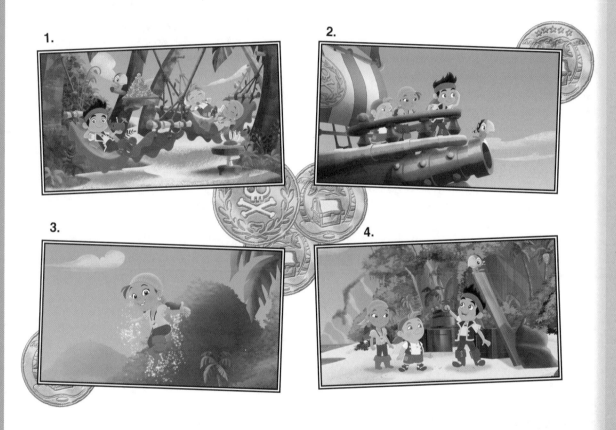

1.

2.

3.

4.

Read these sentences. Are they true or false? Circle the answer.

2. Izzy is in every picture.

true   false

3. Skully is flying in all the pictures.

true   false

Hook is trying to open a mysterious door using Jake's sword as a key. Which shape will Jake's sword fit into?

Answer:

4

In each section, circle your favourite and find out which pirate you are most like.

1. Possession

a. sword

b. map

c. pixie dust

d. Captain Hook's hat

2. Hobby

a. sailing

b. playing harmonica

c. flying

d. napping

3. Catchphrase

a. "Yo-ho! Let's go!"

b. "Aw, coconuts!"

c. "Shiver me timbers!"

d. "I never have any fun!"

Mostly a
You're most like Jake. You're the leader of the crew and always include your best friends in the fun.

Mostly c
You're most like Izzy. You are full of ideas and you always think things through carefully.

Mostly b
You're most like Cubby. You're always rarin' to go-go-GO! You always overcome your fears and act bravely.

Mostly d
Oh dear, you're most like Captain Hook. You're a sneaky snook, who doesn't like to see other people have fun.

At the door, the crew find a message from Peter Pan:
"Only a great leader can open this door,
with an enchanted sword and nothing more."
Look at the clues and write the answers in the grid.
The name of the person who can open the door will
appear in the shaded boxes.

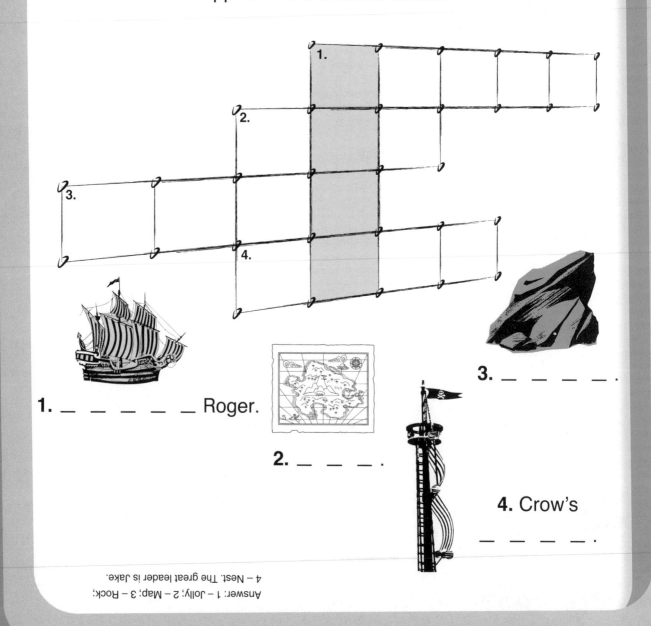

1. _ _ _ _ _ Roger.

2. _ _ _ _ .

3. _ _ _ _ .

4. Crow's _ _ _ _ .

Count the Gold Doubloons and colour them in.

Answer:

8 Gold Doubloons.

Saying what you want to say, but in a pirate way!
Circle the pirate phrases below.

1. "Welcome aboard, me hearties!"

2. "I don't like treasure."

3. "Anchors aweigh!"

4. "Shiver me timbers!"

5. "I always get sea-sick!"

6. "Arrrggh! Fill me boots with barnacles!"

Answers:
1, 3, 4, 6

The Never Land pirates are dancing to a rocking sea shanty.
Colour them in.

Make your own pirate song by circling the words at the end of each verse that you like the most.

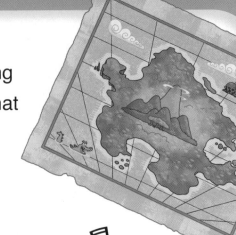

On the shores of Never Land,
There's a pirate crew   *you know!*   *yo-ho!*

For new adventures, they set sail,
Yo-ho!   *Let's go!*   *Let's row!*

Hook, he wants to spoil the fun,
Hear him cry,   *"Avast!"*   *"The last!"*

Jake's pirate crew have fun in the sun,
Every day is such   *a blast!*   *a laugh!*

Colour in your favourite instrument below,
then draw yourself in a pirate band with Cubby.

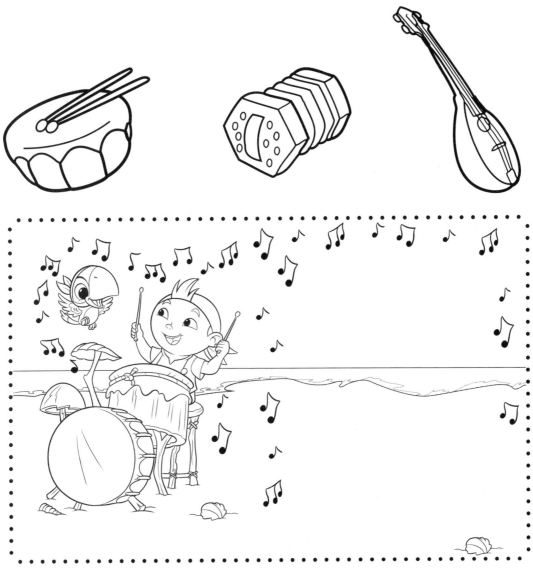

Captain Hook is not happy with the scallywags
who are making that rat-a-tat racket.
Colour him in or walk the plank!

Hook has spotted who is making the noise through his spyglass.
How many music notes can you count?

Answer:
20

Oh, no! Captain Hook and Mr Smee have stolen Cubby's drums. Help Jake and the pirate crew follow the musical notes to the sneaky pirates.

Answer:

These two pirates love to burst into song at the drop of a gang plank. Circle five differences between the two pictures.

Answers:

Join the dots to complete the picture of Never Land.

Draw a line and match each pirate to their shadow.

Answers:
1-C; 2-A;
3-F; 4-E;
5-B; 6-D.

Complete this dot-to-dot of the pirate ship and colour it in.

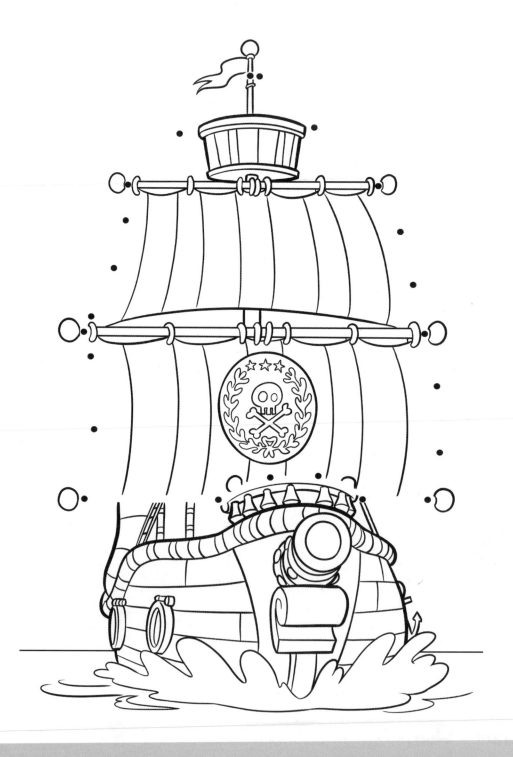

Look at this picture of Captain Hook and Smee.
Find and circle six differences between the two pictures.
Hint: There is one difference in each grid square.

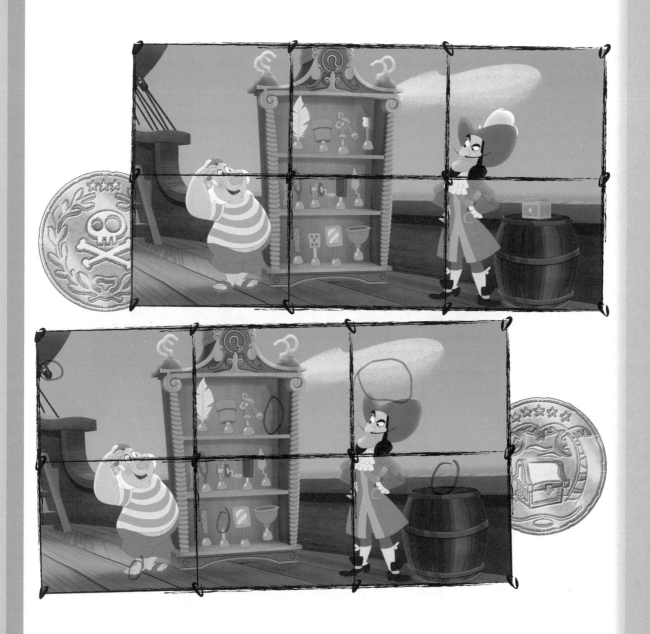

What are Jake, Izzy, Cubby and Skully saying?
Can you trace over the letters to find out?

"Ahoy, mateys!"

"Crackers!"

There's a spooky myth about the golden pumpkin.
The words at the end of each line rhyme.
Circle the rhyming word to complete the myth.

On Halloween eve, the golden pumpkin rises **high**,
In the Never Land **sky/clouds**,
And it starts to **fly/float**.

Can you circle some other words that rhyme with 'high'?

pie   **pirate**

boots   **by**

try   **ship**

135

Which of these shells belongs to Izzy?

Hint: It is different to all the others.

1

2

3

4

5

Answer:

5

Royal Activities!

Sofia is a princess now! Add colour to this picture of her waving to the crowd.

King Roland says there will be a ball in Sofia's honour.
Colour in the scene.

Which picture of Sofia is different to the others?
Circle it!

A

B

C

D

Answer:

B

Colour in the picture of Sofia, Amber and James having a royal tea party.

Sofia has been learning to dance. Complete the number pattern in each row of dance steps.

A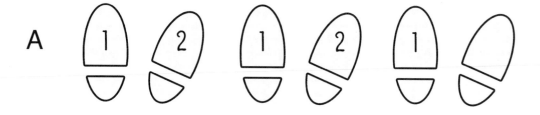

B

C

Cedric is the royal sorcerer. Draw what you imagine he is thinking about today!

Sofia and her friends are having a royal sleepover.
Colour in the scene.

Add some pretty colours to this picture
of Jade and Ruby's princess makeover!

Sofia can't find her way to the dining hall.
Draw a line to lead her through the maze.

START

Join the dots to complete this picture of
a flying horse and then add colour.

Sofia is playing in the palace gardens.
Add colour to this picture of her kicking the ball.

Can you unscramble these names? Look at the pictures for clues!

O F A S I

_ _ _ _ _

E M R B A

_ _ _ _ _

O L I C

_ _ _ _

M E S A J

_ _ _ _ _

Put the pictures of Sofia's morning in order by numbering them 1–4.

A  _____

B  _____

C  _____

D  _____

Answers:
D-1
C-2
B-4
A-3

Sofia is studying in the library. Look at all the books!
Colour the scene.

Time to get up! Add colour to this picture
of Sofia and her forest friends.

Princess Amber and Prince James are twins.
Colour in the scene.

Can you circle four pictures of Sofia?

How many books can you count?

books
_____

Colour in this picture of Sofia, Amber and James as they fly to Royal Prep in the royal coach.

Add colour to Flora, Fauna and Merryweather.
They are headmistresses at Royal Prep.

Can you circle seven items that begin with the letter 'b'?

Draw lines to link Sofia, James and Amber to their shadows.

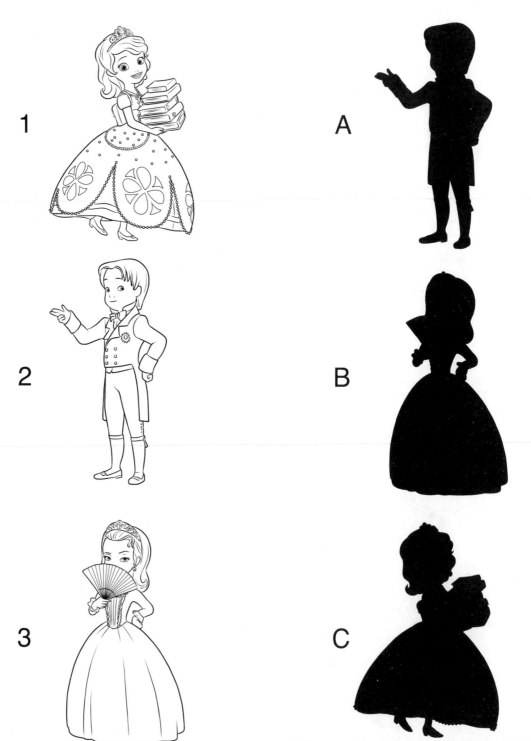

1

2

3

A

B

C

Answers:

Sofia is dancing with King Roland at the grand ball.
Colour in the scene.

There are six differences between these two pictures.
Can you spot them?

Answers:

Sofia and her flying horse, Minimus, are winning the race!
Add colour as they cross the finish line.

The table is set for a royal banquet.
Can you count the tableware?

How many forks do you see? _6_

How many knives do you see? _3_

How many spoons do you see? _3_

Draw your dream castle, then colour it in.

Amber is helping Sofia learn some new dance steps before the royal ball. Colour in the scene.

Sofia loves to draw and paint. Add colour to this picture of Sofia and her friend Vivian in art class.

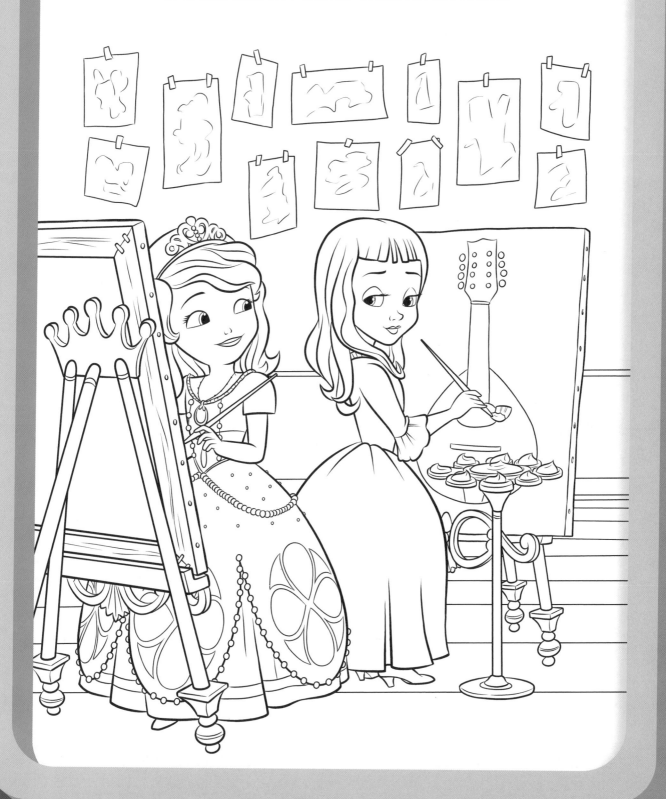

Can you circle five pictures of Crackle, the dragon?

How many magic wands can you count?

 magic wands

Join the dots to complete Sofia's pretty hairstyle
and then add colour.

Baileywick is ringing the bell –
dinner is served! Colour in the scene.

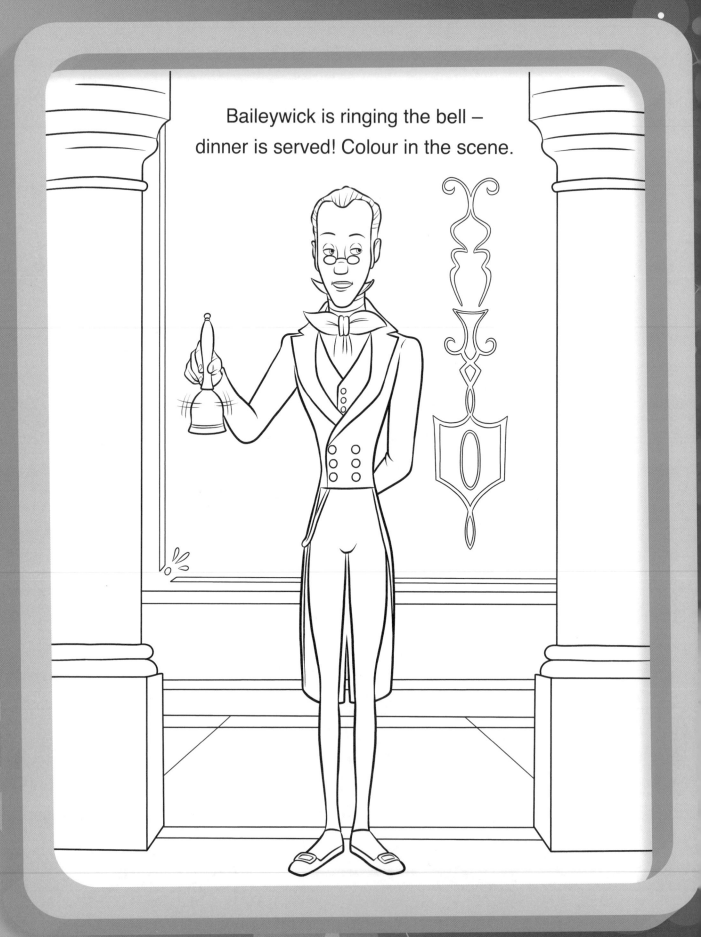

Sofia is walking in the forest.
Can you circle ten creatures in the picture?

Answers:

169

Sofia is learning magic! Add colour to this picture of her practising a spell.

Help Sofia and Minimus reach the finish line.
Find the right path through the maze!

START

FINISH

Answer:

King Roland has a special present for Sofia –
a magical amulet! Colour in the scene.

Cedric mixes many potions. Add colour to this picture of him in his lab.

How many flying horses can you count?

Answer: 14

Sofia loves her new family and being a princess!
Add colour to this picture of the royal family.

Princess Sofia is dressed up for the royal ball.
Colour in the scene.

The Royal
Slumber Party

Written by Catherine Hapka • Based on an episode by Erica Rothschild
Illustrated by Character Building Studio and the Disney Storybook Artists

Sofia and Amber are having a royal sleepover tonight!
"This is where we'll be sleeping," Amber says.
"The observatory? We'll sleep under the stars!" Sofia cries.
"It's a royal slumber party," Amber says. "Everything has to be amazing."

The royal herald's trumpet sounds.

"Our friends are here!" Sofia cries.

Amber's two friends, Princess Hildegard and Princess Clio, step out of their coaches. Behind them are Jade and Ruby in an oxcart.

"I can't believe we're here!" Jade exclaims, hugging Sofia.

"We're so excited!" Ruby adds.

Once everyone has put on their nightgowns,
Ruby and Jade twist their hair with pine cone rollers.
The other princesses stare at them.
"What are they wearing?" Hildegard says.
"What are they doing?" Clio wonders.
Amber frowns. "Are those pine cones?"
Ruby hears her and dances over. "Do you want one?
We brought extras."

Amber marches over to Sofia. "Sofia! Pine cones are not part of a perfect princess slumber party."

Sofia is worried. She wants her new sister and her old friends to like each other.

"They can fit in, Amber," she says. "They just need a little help."

Sofia has a great idea. "How would you two like a royal makeover?" she asks her friends.

Ruby and Jade squeal with excitement!

Baileywick and Sofia's woodland friends help out. They fix the girls' hair and dress them in pretty gowns and sparkling tiaras.

Sofia makes her friends cover their eyes. Then she leads them to a mirror. "Open your eyes," she says.

Jade and Ruby gasp when they see themselves.

"I'm a princess!" Ruby exclaims.

"Me, too!" cries Jade.

Now it's time for party activities.
First comes fan decorating.
    Ruby and Jade have fun, but their
fans don't look very princessy.

Next the girls play a game of Pin the Tail
on the Unicorn.
    "Ooh! Ooh!" Jade says. "Can I go first?"
    But Jade ends up nowhere
near the unicorn!

Then the girls watch Cedric, the royal sorcerer, put on a magic puppet show in the banquet hall. During the show, James, Sofia's brother, walks in with a message for the girls.

"Prince James!" Jade and Ruby cry, rushing towards him. They're thrilled to see the friendly prince!

Jade and Ruby are so excited that they accidentally knock over the chocolate-milk fountain. Oops!

Chocolate milk splashes on to Amber's nightgown. She is furious!

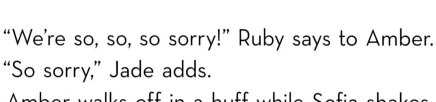

"We're so, so, so sorry!" Ruby says to Amber.
"So sorry," Jade adds.
 Amber walks off in a huff while Sofia shakes her head sadly.

Baileywick hurries Jade and Ruby away to get cleaned up. Then James tells the girls it's time for some dancing in the throne room.

"Let's go," Amber says. "Maybe we can enjoy five minutes of our party without Sofia's friends making a mess."

Now Sofia is even more worried! She goes to find her friends.

"I just want you both to fit in with the princesses," Sofia explains.

"We look just like them now, don't we?" Jade asks.

"Yes," Sofia says. "But princesses don't talk as much, or laugh as loud, or make as much mess."

Jade frowns. "We were just having fun."

"We're sorry," Ruby adds quickly. "We'll try to act more like Amber and the other princesses."

"Thank you!" Sofia is relieved. Now she's sure everyone will get along!

Sofia and her friends join the others in the throne room. But Ruby and Jade don't know how to waltz. All they can do is stand there and watch the four princesses dance.

After a while, they tell Sofia that they would like to go home.

"But you're finally fitting in!" Sofia cries. "And you're not embarrassing me!"

"I'm sorry if we talk too much and laugh too loudly for your fancy new friends," says Jade. "Maybe we shouldn't be friends any more!"

Ruby takes Jade's arm and together they rush
out of the room.

"Don't worry about them," Hildegard tells Sofia.
"You're with us now."

Sofia goes after her friends but finds her mother instead. "I was trying to help Jade and Ruby fit in," she explains. "But I made them feel bad."

"A true princess treats people with kindness, Sofia," Queen Miranda says gently. "If someone is your friend, you should like them for who they are."

Sofia knows her mother is right. She runs outside and finds her friends as they are about to leave.

"I'm sorry about the way I acted," she says. "Please let me make it up to you. We can have our own slumber party – just the three of us!"

Jade and Ruby think for a moment and then finally agree to stay.

Soon Sofia and her friends are in her room having
a great time. They laugh – loudly! They talk – a lot!
They roll pine cones in their hair and put tiaras on top.

Meanwhile, Amber and her friends go back to the observatory.
"Finally, it's just us princesses," Amber says.
"This is a perfect party," Hildegard agrees with a yawn.
There's a long silence. The princesses are really bored.
"You know," Clio says, "Sofia's friends were kind of fun."

A moment later, Amber and her friends knock on Sofia's door.

"Um, do you have room for a few more princesses?" asks Amber.

Sofia looks at Jade and Ruby. "What do you think?"

"The more, the merrier," Ruby says with a smile.

Sofia and Amber end up having the perfect sleepover with friends – old and new!

The End

FOLLOW THAT SOUND!

WRITTEN BY **MELINDA LA ROSE**

ILLUSTRATED BY **ALAN BATSON**

One day on Shipwreck Beach, Cubby is playing his harmonica.

"Aw, coconuts! I'll never be ready in time to play at Marina's party," says Cubby sadly.

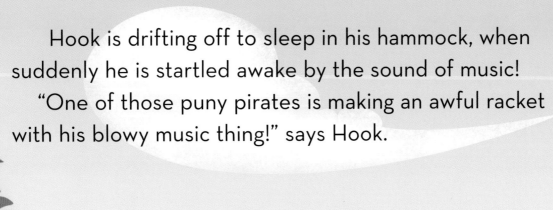

Hook is drifting off to sleep in his hammock, when suddenly he is startled awake by the sound of music! "One of those puny pirates is making an awful racket with his blowy music thing!" says Hook.

"Why don't you ask the sea pups nicely if they'll be a little quieter?" says Smee.

"Smee, who do you think you're dealing with?" says Hook.

"Why would I ask nicely when I can take the blowy thing away!"

Hook uses his fishing hook to nab the harmonica right out of Cubby's mouth!

Swoosh!

"My harmonica!" says Cubby.
"We gotta get it back!" says Jake.

Smee blows into the harmonica. It makes a terrible noise!

Weeeee-yooouuu!

Startled, Smee throws the harmonica up in the air ...
but it doesn't come back down!

"Um, Cap'n," says Smee, "the
harmonica just disappeared!"

"Crackers!" says Skully. "That monkey took the harmonica!"

"He's heading for the Never Jungle," says Cubby.

"Come on, crew," says Jake. "Follow that monkey!"

"But how?" asks Cubby.
"We can swing on the vines just like the monkey!" says Izzy.
"Uh-oh," says Skully. "I lost sight of him!"

Just then, the crew hears music!
"It's my harmonica," says Cubby.
"Follow that sound!" says Jake.

207

"Hi, Mr Monkey," says Jake. "I'm glad you like the harmonica, but it belongs to my friend Cubby."
"And I need it to practise for the big party tonight!" adds Cubby.

"He doesn't want to give the harmonica back," says Izzy.
"If only we had another instrument," says Jake. "Then we could trade with the monkey."
"That's a great idea," says Izzy.

"We can make an instrument for the monkey to play.
Now we need something to put inside," says Izzy.
She picks up two coconuts.
"I found some rocks," says Cubby.
"I've got some shells," says Skully.
"Perfect," says Izzy.

"Awesome! You made maracas for the monkey," says Jake.

The monkey gives Cubby back his harmonica.

"Thanks!" says Cubby. "Hey, do you wanna come back to Shipwreck Beach and jam with me?"

"Oo-oo-oo," says the happy monkey.

Cubby and the monkey play music together on the beach.

"Blast it, now there's twice as much racket!" says Captain Hook.

"What's the matter?" asks Jake.

"The Cap'n can't have his nappy-nap, what with all that music," says Smee.

"Why didn't you just ask us to be quieter?" asks Jake.

"But, how can I practise for the party?" says Cubby.

"I've got an idea," says Jake.

Cubby and the monkey play a gentle lullaby for Captain Hook. Mr Smee sings:

"Cap'n, close your weary eyes.
Now it's time for beddy-byes.
The music's sweet; it's not too shabby.
When you wake up, you won't be crabby."

Hook falls asleep and starts to snore loudly!
"We'd better get ready for the party," says Jake.
"What? I can't hear you over all that noise," says Skully.

Later that night, Cubby and the monkey play their instruments at Marina's party!

"Cubby, thank you so much for playing," says Marina. "You were amazing!"

"You're welcome," says Cubby, blushing.

"Yo-ho, way to go!" says Jake. "See? All that practising paid off!"

"Can't you hear it, Smee?" says Captain Hook.

"Hear what, Cap'n?" asks Smee.

"That blasted lullaby. I can't get it out of me head," says Hook.

"Oh dear, you're imagining things, Cap'n," says Smee.

"I guess I am," says Hook.

"I can see why. It was a very catchy tune, if I do say so myself," says Smee. "And the lyrics were top-notch."

Uh-oh! The monkey has stowed away on the *Jolly Roger*!

"If Hook had just asked us to be quiet, we wouldn't have gone through all that trouble today," says Jake.

"Yeah, Hook should know better! If you need something, you should ask nicely," says Izzy.

"Yeah, but if the monkey hadn't taken the harmonica, we never would've got to jam together!" says Cubby.

The End